NINJA
FARTS

NINJA FARTS

THE DISGUSTING ADVENTURES OF MILO SNOTROCKET

J. B. O'NEIL

Sky Pony Press
New York

Sky Pony Press books may be purchased in bulk at special discounts for sales promotion, corporate gifts, fund-raising, or educational purposes. Special editions can also be created to specifications. For details, contact the Special Sales Department, Sky Pony Press, 307 West 36th Street, 11th Floor, New York, NY 10018 or info@ skyhorsepublishing.com.

Sky Pony® is a registered trademark of Skyhorse Publishing, Inc.®, a Delaware corporation.

Visit our website at www.skyponypress.com.

10 9 8 7 6 5 4 3 2 1

Library of Congress Cataloging-in-Publication Data is available on file.

Cover design by Michael Short
Cover and interior illustrations by J. B. O'Neil

Print ISBN: 978-1-5107-2435-8
Ebook ISBN: 978-1-5107-2437-2

Printed in Canada

TABLE OF CONTENTS

A Crazy, Stinky Dream 7

Why I Hate My Alarm Clock 8

I Blame My Mom...10

The Bully on the Bus 12

The Bus Is Kinda Fun 13

Just Another Day at School...............................14

Weird Science Class...16

Can't . . . Stay . . . Awake 18

Me . . . Ninja Fart Master! 19

The Terrible Fart King 20

Can't Pay the Fart Tax?....................................21

Flattened By the Flatulator................................22

The Ancient Art of Fart Fu...............................24

Ninja Farts to the Rescue! 25

But Was it All a Dream?...................................26

One Noise Hid the Other..................................27

What Would a Fart Ninja Do? 28

Following Bobby Buttz-Cratcher 30

Bottled Farts Are Pure Evil...............................32

Farts Are My Destiny 34

Bullies = No Match for Fart Fu.........................36

Mercy Farts..38

Summoning the Ancient "Dragon Fart"...........40

Horrible Farts Save the Day! 42

An Important Speech About Farting.................44

A Bully Sees the Error of His Ways 46

Using Farts For Good . . . NOT For Evil.........48

The Element of Surprise......................................50

My Stinky Apprentice..52

The Training Begins...54

The Stinger...56

Practice Makes Perfect 58

The Mystical Fart Bomb 60

The Dark Night...62

Bobby's Final Test 64

Let the Battle Begin! 66

Bobby, Fart Ninja...68

Two Farts Are Better Than One! 70

We're on TV! 72

Fame At Last!..73

Even Mom Didn't Recognize Me! 74

Keeping a Low Profile..76

The Name Game 78

Day Off? Ha! 79

Big Fart and Farter Starter to the Rescue 80

Whoever Smelt It, Dealt It...................................82

Let 'Em Rip!...83

Urgh, the Taste! 84

Gentlemen Ninjas..85

The Whole School Is Suddenly Full of Ninjas 86

Ninjas Get BUS-ted...88

Is It a Bus or a Plane?..89

The Bus Balloon 90

100 Milos Per Hour...92

And Home We Go..94

Back to Normal 95

A CRAZY, STINKY DREAM . . .

Oh no! There are so many enemy ninjas chasing me.

I started jumping from tree to tree, leaping so fast that the forest turned into a green blur. I need to think of something fast! I am a ninja, what do ninjas do in this situation?

They remember their teachings.

My master always told me the way of the ninja is to be as sneaky as possible, but when that doesn't work, create a fart cloud so smelly and thick that nobody could possibly follow you. So that's what I did. As I ran, I focused all of my energy into making the stinkiest, smelliest, most eye-watering nose-burning butt rocket I could. I flew forward on my green fart jet leaving the other ninjas gagging. I could hear them coughing and yelling to each other— *BEEP BEEP BEEP BEEP!*

WHY I HATE
MY ALARM CLOCK

Ugh, stupid alarm clock. That was the best dream I'd ever had.

"Milo! Milo!" My mom called up the stairs. "Milo!"

She was making sure I was awake. Isn't that what alarms are for?

"I'm awake!" I yelled back.

My room smelled terrible. I must have been sleep farting again. I guess if you fart in your dreams, you fart in real life. I got out of bed and got dressed for school. Mom would be mad if I was late again. The problem was that my stomach was making some gurgly noises. I guess I didn't quite get all the farts out in my dream. I farted so loud and powerfully that I flew down the stairs.

I BLAME MY MOM

Oh man, it's fun coming down the stairs at warp speed! I wondered if I could apply to the International Space Program to be the first boy launched into space by fart fuel? Hmm . . . I barely had time to think these thoughts because it only took a nanosecond to reach the bottom.

Oof. I landed on something soft. Something soft and . . . *smelly!* I must have hit my head on the way down because I was sure I'd have noticed letting out a fart that smelled that bad. Then the soft floor beneath me started to move, and I realized I'd landed on my dog, Pooter. The force of my fart-propelled body landing on his tummy had forced a huge dog fart out, and boy did it smell bad. I'd have been proud of that one!

My mom looked super crabby as I sat down for breakfast.

"Milo, you know how I feel about farting," she said. "Farting is gross and rude, and you should stop doing it."

My mom doesn't understand.

"Mom, I can't just *stop* farting. I have to fart. It's who I am." She's a mom; it's not her fault that she doesn't get it. I sat down at the table and waited for breakfast. She brought me a plate full of eggs and beans. My mom *really* doesn't get it.

THE BULLY
ON THE BUS

I ate my breakfast and went outside to wait for the bus. My stomach was already telling me that this was going to be a farty day. I just hoped Bobby Buttz-Cratcher wasn't there. He was the meanest kid I knew.

I got on the bus as it pulled up and oh boy, Bobby was there, farting. He actually grabbed another kid's face and farted into it so hard that Bobby flew into his seat. He left a fart trail floating in the air behind him, sort of like a shooting star. It was beautiful in a gross green-fart-trail kind of way. The poor kid who got his face farted into was completely knocked out with his head in a gas cloud.

THE BUS
IS KINDA FUN

The bus pulled into its usual spot, next to the parking lot where all the kids who don't ride the bus get dropped off by their parents. Sometimes I wish my mom would take me to school, but then I'd miss all the farting fun on the bus and I kinda think it'd be boring, even though I hated it when Bobby Buttz-Cratcher picked on me. Once, on the way to school, he sat on my head and farted. That stuff was so bad I could chew it like gum! I swear, every time I breathed out for the rest of that day, my mouth smelt like Bobby Buttz-Cratcher's butt.

It had its advantages, though. One of our teachers, Mrs. Shufflebottom, has a habit of leaning in so far when she's talking to you that her nose touches yours. All it took was one whiff of my Bobby-scented breath, and she hasn't spoken to me since. It's great!

JUST ANOTHER DAY AT SCHOOL

We pulled in front of the school. This was the moment we all waited for every morning. The moment when the doors of the bus opened and the smell got out in front of us. The driver of the bus wouldn't open the doors until we were all behaving, so Bobby Buttz-Cratcher would play until he could see some parents walking past the bus. Then he would stop messing around so the driver would open the doors.

If he timed it just right, the parents would walk *right* into a huge cloud of farty gas. Sometimes it was yellow, and sometimes it would be orange, depending on what the gassiest kids had been eating. But the mom or dad walking into it would always go the same color—green—right before they passed out on the sidewalk.

WEIRD SCIENCE CLASS

My day always starts with science class. Science and Bobby. It's a good thing science is so cool, because this teacher is so boring. The class was full of beakers filled with bubbling chemicals and strange fumes floating out of the tops of most of them, but we were all stuck listening to Mr. Figgins drone on and on about something. I didn't really know. He was too boring to listen to. I started getting so sleepy, but I don't even think he noticed what we kids were doing anyway. He just loved to talk.

I almost always fall asleep in Mr. Figgins's class. Actually, I almost always fall asleep in most classes. Sometimes his lesson is fun and he'd blow stuff up. But most of the time he just talked. Today, I had to fight it. Mom had given me so many beans that morning, *and* an extra egg. I was concentrating hard on holding it in. And, as I already knew from the smell of my bedroom when I woke up this morning, I sleep-fart. A lot.

CAN'T...STAY...AWAKE

I could feel my eyelids getting heavy sitting at my desk. School is so boring sometimes that no matter how hard I try, I just can't stay awake. I don't think teachers will ever understand. Then, just as I was falling asleep, I heard Bobby say something to the kid next to him.

"It's finally done. I've figured out the perfect recipe for my farts. I've been working on them for months in science class and now they're done! These farts that I've made smell so bad that they'll burn your nose-hair out! No one will be able to stand them."

ME . . . NINJA FART MASTER!

Even that news couldn't keep me awake today, though. I felt myself falling into the dream world, where I was once again a ninja, this time standing outside a giant castle. I had to get inside and I had to go unseen, as ninjas must. This fortress seemed impossible to get into, but there were no walls that could keep this fart ninja out. I snuck up to the front gate, hidden by the dark night.

THE TERRIBLE FART KING

At the front, there was a group of armed guards making sure nobody got in or out. I ran up the walls and jumped over the guards, and made my way to the throne room. When I got there I saw King Bobby Buttz-Cratcher sitting in his throne yelling at his subjects.

"I need more farts! My people aren't paying the fart tax! How is my kingdom supposed to function without the farts?" Bobby slammed his hands on his throne and stood up. He pointed at a frail old man who was on his knees, "Where are my farts, you? You're late on your fart tax!"

CAN'T PAY THE FART TAX?

The old man stood in front of Bobby, shaking from head to toe.

"Please King Bobby, my family has farted all we can for you. We don't have any farts left. My family is all out of farts," the old man explained.

"All out of farts? There are always more farts, and you will give them to me now." King Bobby stood up and walked towards the old man until he was standing over him. "I know you have more farts in you, and I know how to get them all out! Every single last fart. Guards, bring out the Flatulator!"

FLATTENED BY THE FLATULATOR

The guards walked into another room. They came out from the darkness a few moments later, wheeling in a contraption that looked like a giant rolling pin.

"Guards, put him through it. He will pay his fart tax one way or another," King Bobby declared.

"Please King Bobby," the old man pleaded. "Please. I don't have any farts left. If I did, I would give them to you. Don't put me through the Flatulator!" But it was no use. The guards grabbed him and put him in front of the Flatulator.

"Get me those farts!" said King Bobby. They began to roll the machine over the old man from head to foot, flattening him like a pancake. By the end of it, the tiniest poots escaped the man and were caught in a jar.

"I knew he was lying. There are always more farts. Now get him out of here." The guards scraped the old man off the ground with shovels and threw him into another room.

THE ANCIENT ART OF FART FU

I saw the whole thing from the shadows, but I couldn't think of how to stop him in time. The poor old man never had a chance. It was over. The only thing that I could do now was make sure that he never did anything like this again. Using the ancient teachings of Fart Fu, I mustered up some gas. I focused my digestive tract and thought ninja star thoughts, and from my butt, gas seeped out slowly and surely.

I made ninja fart stars and got ready to throw them. They may have been made of gas, but they were as solid as anything handcrafted by the ninjas themselves. I made two and I knew that when I threw these, I could not miss. These stars had to fly true and had to hit their targets.

NINJA FARTS TO THE RESCUE!

I closed my eyes and focused on my throw to come. I opened my eyes and threw my ninja fart stars straight at King Bobby. They flew through the air leaving a gas trail behind them. My aim was good. The two fart stars each hit their target, one under each one of the evil king's nostrils.

"What's this?" The King yelled. "The smell! The smell is so bad! These are—these are the worst farts I've ever smelled in my life! With this power I could rule the world!"

The two stars exploded into a cloud of green gas with so much force that it knocked him over and he fell on his butt. "These farts . . ." he mumbled before he passed out from the terrible smell. I knew that there was nobody—not even an evil king of farts—that could stand such a smell. The cloud around his head got bigger and bigger. This was the way of the ninja.

BUT WAS IT ALL A DREAM?

All of a sudden my head felt like it was falling really fast towards a very hard surface that I really didn't want it to hit. *THWUNK!*

Oh, man! I woke up from my dream because my head fell off my hand and slammed into my desk so hard it made a loud noise that everyone could hear.

"Mr. Snotrocket," Mr. Figgins said. "Now that you seem to be done sleeping, can you please tell me the answer to the question on the board?"

Oh, boy. "Uhh," I said, "Can you repeat the question?"

Mr. Figgins sighed. "Mr. Snotrocket, can you please explain how I am supposed to repeat a question for you that is already written?" he asked. I stammered something out, but didn't really say anything. All the other kids in the class laughed at me. Man, I looked stupid.

ONE NOISE HID THE OTHER

Even though my head hurt from banging it hard on the desk, I was grateful for it. As my forehead made contact, the jolt dislodged the eggy, beany gas in my stomach. In that split second, the seat of my pants lifted into the air as a huge fart escaped. But the *THWUNK* of my head butt, along with the other kids laughing, hid the sound.

Nobody suspected a thing, and because it came out with such force, it landed right among the other kids and nobody could tell who it belonged to. Farting in Mr. Figgins's class always landed the kid responsible in trouble. Let me tell you, sitting in school during recess, writing "I must not flatulate in class" one hundred times, is not fun. Especially when the window in Mr. Figgins's classroom looked out on to the school yard, and I could see the other kids holding their noses as they had a farting contest.

WHAT WOULD A FART NINJA DO?

RIIIING!

I was so disoriented that when the bell rang, I could hardly believe that class was over already. I guess I did accidentally sleep through just about the whole thing. Oh well.

As I was putting my books into my backpack, I saw something that made the hair on the back of my neck stand up: Bobby putting jars filled with green and yellow gas into his backpack. He was looking around, making sure nobody saw what he was doing, and it looked like he thought he got away with it, but luckily I saw him.

I had a feeling in my gut that something really weird was about to happen with Bobby and those gassy jars of gunk. What would a real ninja do in this situation? What should I do? The problem was, I've only dreamt about being a ninja, and I've never actually put the mask on to fight with the power of my butt in "real life" before. I just didn't know if I could do it. All of these thoughts bounced around my head like a fart in a mitten, and I was suddenly paralyzed by not knowing what to do next.

FOLLOWING BOBBY BUTTZ-CRATCHER

I decided that I should follow Bobby to see what his next move would be. I mean, he might not even do anything, so there would be no reason for me to become a ninja in the first place. I followed him through the hallways, walking behind other kids, moving as they moved, stepping where they stepped. I became their shadow. I knew that if Bobby saw me following him, I would be lucky if he only beat me up. It was a good thing I was so good at sneaking. I guess if you spend enough time practicing to be a ninja, you actually get pretty good at it. Cool, huh?

BOTTLED FARTS
ARE PURE EVIL

Bobby stopped outside the girls' locker room, surrounded by his group of cronies.

"Hey Bobby, what do you got for us in there?" asked one of the group. They were all looking as Bobby took off his backpack and opened it so that the rest of the group could look into it. Bobby started laughing while he scratched his butt and showed off what he had.

"Check it out guys, I made this in science class. It's jarred farts. They smell way worse than anything that a person could fart out. Science rocks, guys. You should really try harder so you can do this, too."

I was watching this from behind a wall. What do I do here? A ninja would stop him.

"I'm going to open these and throw them into the girls' locker room. It's going to smell so bad and everybody will think that the girls all farted. It'll be the funniest thing that ever happened at this lame school, and everyone's going to blame the girls. It's the perfect crime!"

FARTS ARE
MY DESTINY . . .

Whoa. Wait . . . back up. What did Bobby just say? That he was going to throw the fart jars into the girls' locker room? If he did that, the smell would be the last of the girls' worries. I knew I had to do something, otherwise those girls would be stepping all over the broken glass. Bobby Buttz-Cratcher might have been okay at science, but he wasn't too bright when it came to life. Blaming the bad smell on the girls was one thing, but this could get really bad. I knew what I had to do.

I walked to the boys' locker room. It already smelled like farts in here. I walked up to my locker and opened it, revealing my ninja outfit. I had been bringing it to school everyday for a year, just in case I ever had the courage to put it on and be a hero.

A true hero would don the mask and save the day, but I wasn't sure if I was a true hero. Just dreaming about being a hero doesn't mean you are one. A real hero is defined by their actions. They do heroic things because heroic things need to be done.

I wasn't sure if I had that courage inside me. I was so scared, but then I remembered something my dad once told me: "Courage is not about being fearless, it is about doing what is right, even if you're scared." Then I knew what I had to do. I took the costume out of my locker and became the fart ninja. I became the hero I needed to be. I became the hero that *everybody* needed me to be.

BULLIES = NO MATCH FOR FART FU

I came out of the boys' locker room. I emerged unnoticed by the other kids in the hall and snuck up behind Bobby. I got behind him and tapped him on the shoulder. He jumped and turned around.

"Who do you think you are, kid? Nobody touches Bobby Buttz-Cratcher. Especially not some kid wearing a stupid ninja outfit," he yelled. Then he pushed me in the chest. I didn't realize how much bigger he was than me until he was right in front of me, pushing me. I was so scared.

"I'm the fart ninja, Bobby. I am a master of Fart Fu, and I know what you're planning to do. A real ninja would never let you get away with such an evil plan!" I was almost shaking because of how scared I was.

"Then it's a good thing there's not a real ninja around to try and stop me," he replied. Then he and all the kids around him started laughing.

"That is where you are wrong, Bobby. I am a real ninja, and no words can stop me from doing what's right. I will stop you, Bobby. I will stop you!"

MERCY FARTS

Bobby's cronies were still laughing, even though some of them looked a bit scared. I mean, it's not every day that a ninja turns up at the school. We had had a talk once in school about bullies, and how the kids who hang around with them only do it because they'd rather have the bully as a friend than an enemy. And because they think it makes them look tough. As I stood there, in my fart ninja outfit, I noticed a few of them taking a step back. That gave me strength, and I puffed out my chest to make myself look bigger. I was a fart ninja, and I was going to beat this mortal enemy. I took a deep breath . . .

Then I focused all of my energy to my butt and let loose. A giant fart cloud erupted from me, blinding and gagging all of the kids around me. I made sure to hold back on the stinkiness so that none of the innocent witnesses were hurt. I made sure to make it extra thick, though, so that no one saw as I rocketed up into the air on a fart jet.

When I got to the ceiling, I made an extra thick cloud out of farts and sat on it. I floated on it and tried to figure out my next move. Bobby was so much bigger and stronger than me. I had to remember everything I had learned, all of my ninja teachings.

SUMMONING THE ANCIENT "DRAGON FART"

BZTPPTB

I didn't have long to come up with my next move. One of the most important lessons of the ninja teachings is that farts only have power while they're still hot. The hotter they come out, the stronger they are. My extra thick cloud fart had burned, so I knew I still had time, but I had to think fast. As my cloud started to cool down, I closed my eyes, and thought my most powerful ninja thoughts.

What was I taught? What is the ultimate ninja technique? Then it hit me. The single most powerful ninja technique that there is. I had to use it. I sat on my cloud and began to summon it. I began a long series of farts, molding them into one thing. I wove them together through the air, sticking them together in intricate and elaborate ways, creating a work of fart art. The great masters themselves could have made nothing more beautiful than what I had. Before I knew it, my masterpiece was complete.

It was a giant dragon made of farts! It was the embodiment of all of the teachings of the ninja: silent, but deadly!

HORRIBLE FARTS SAVE THE DAY!

The dragon struck from the shadows. I sent it right at Bobby. If I missed, there was a chance that it could attack the wrong person. This dragon contained all of my ninja strength and was very difficult to control. I mean, this thing was a dragon; it had a mind of its own. I could guide it, I could tell it what to do, but if it decided on another target, it would go after them. I gave it all of the information I could as I was making it, and I trusted it to make the right choice and take down Bobby.

The dragon struck from the shadows and did the right thing. It flew down and swallowed Bobby and his backpack full of farts up whole. It flew around the hallways until it farted out Bobby and his now empty backpack.

All of the farts in Bobby's backpack had gotten out of their jars. The dragon turned Bobby and his jars of farts into its own fart, and it farted him out. Bobby was lying on the ground, dazed. All of his hair burned off because of how bad the inside of the fart dragon smelled. All of the other kids covered their faces because they couldn't handle how bad Bobby smelled now.

AN IMPORTANT SPEECH ABOUT FARTING

I jumped off of my fart cloud and walked over to Bobby, who was still lying on the ground.

"Bobby, I am very sorry that it came to this, but I had to stop you. You forced me to stop you. You were using farts for the purposes of evil, but farts are supposed to be used for good. Farts are amazing, wonderful things. Everybody farts. Your mom farts, your teachers fart, and even girls fart. There is nobody on earth right now who doesn't fart. To use farts for the purposes of evil makes something that we all do bad. It makes us all bad. If we use them for the forces of good, then we can make everybody better. We can make the whole world better.

"Remember this, Bobby: No matter how good you think you are at being evil, there will always be a fart ninja there to stop you. We defend the Order of Farts. We protect farts and the goodness that they all have in them. Some people say they're gross, and some of them are, but we will do everything we can to protect them."

Bobby stared up at me the whole time. His eyes even started to water, and I don't think it was because of the smell.

A BULLY SEES THE ERROR OF HIS WAYS

Bobby started to talk, but at first it seemed like he was having some trouble getting all of the words out.

"I-I'm so sorry. It's just that, because of my name, other kids used to make fun of me all the time, so I thought that the only thing that I could do to make them stop was to bully them before they even had the chance. I don't want to be a bully; I'm just so scared that other kids are going to make fun of me before they even get to know me.

"I'm really not a bad guy deep down; I just don't want other kids to hurt my feelings. I just thought that because everybody likes farts so much, if I figured out how to make them, then everybody would like me. I'm really sorry. I just wanted to be one of the guys. I just wanted to fit in and have everybody else finally like me. I guess I did it wrong."

USING FARTS FOR GOOD . . . NOT FOR EVIL

I had no idea that Bobby was such a complex person. I had just assumed that he was a bully because he was just a bad kid. I guess even bullies are still just kids trying to be happy, just like the rest of us. Bobby kept apologizing, over and over again. I held up a hand to stop him.

"Bobby, I am sorry. I underestimated you. I didn't give you a chance to prove that you were a good person deep down. Clearly you are, and because of that, I am going to give you a second chance. Today I saw great fart potential in you. In fact, you have enough potential to possibly join the ninja fart order. If you vow to me right now that from now on you will only use your natural fart talent for the powers of good, I will train you."

I offered him my hand to help him stand up and get off the ground. He stood up and looked at me. His eyes were filling up with tears of joy.

"Thank you so much, strange ninja! I swear I'll be good. You're right, farts are amazing, and all I want to do is use them to make the world a better place for everyone! I'll train harder than anyone you ever met. I'll be the best fart ninja ever! But I just gotta know—who are you?"

I took my mask off and looked at Bobby.

"You can call me Milo."

THE ELEMENT
OF SURPRISE

Bobby looked at me as I stood with my mask in my hand. His mouth hung open so far the school bus could have driven right in!

"It's you!" he spluttered.

I nodded. "Yes, Bobby, it is me, Milo Snotrocket. I am a fart ninja, student of the Ninja Fart Order and doer of good deeds." I stood solemnly, waiting for Bobby to speak.

"B-but you're that kid in my class. The goofy kid I sat on in the bus that time." Again I nodded, in what I hoped was a wise way.

"Bobby, fart ninjas hold no grudges. We know that kids can go down the wrong path and use their farting skills for bad things. Yes, it was my head you sat on, and my mouth you farted in, but that time has passed. Now it is my job to turn your skills to good use."

Bobby came towards me. At first I thought he was going to hold me down and fart in my mouth again, but then I realized he had something much worse in mind. Bobby Buttz-Cratcher was going to hug me! I stepped aside just in time. I may be a ninja, but there are some things that I just can't do, and one of them was to hug Bobby Buttz-Cratcher.

"Milo, will you teach me everything that you know, so that I can be a fart ninja, too? I promise, I'll do anything you say. Please, please teach me what you know so that I can use my farting powers for good instead of evil!"

I looked at him with my best super-ninja master look, put my hand on his shoulder, and said "Yes, Grasshopper. We start training tomorrow."

MY STINKY APPRENTICE

I never thought I'd be training a Fart Fu apprentice to join me as a martial fartist in the super-secret Ninja Farts Order, but Bobby Buttz-Cratcher turned out to be an excellent student. Of course, Bobby had a lot to learn about the ways of the Fart Ninja, because he had no idea how to harness the true power of his farts.

First of all, he was terrible at controlling the stink factor—different situations required different levels of disgustingness after all. Then there was the issue of volume—Bobby hadn't quite perfected the "silent-but-violent" method required when the element of surprise is crucial to the success of a mission. Also, he was nowhere near ready in the art of fart directing—I mean, it's no good trying to stop a robber in his tracks by farting in the other direction and temporarily blinding the little old lady who is standing behind us.

But—or should I say *butt*—I knew that he had potential, and a true Fart Fu Master never gives up on an apprentice.

THE TRAINING BEGINS

Every day after school, Bobby and I would train together, and I slowly revealed the secrets of the Fart Ninja. Of course, nobody knew I was a Fart Ninja, not even my mom, so the training had to be performed in a top-secret location, and with military precision.

I also had to complete all of my homework during study hall, so that my mom wouldn't get suspicious of what I was really doing when I disappeared for hours after school.

On the bright side, Mom was super impressed with my new homework habits.

"Milo, I am so proud of you, doing your homework even before you get home from school every day! What's gotten into you? And I haven't seen you turn the TV on for days!"

I felt kinda guilty, letting her think I was just being super-enthusiastic about school, but it was all for the greater good. The world needed another Fart Ninja, and with (a lot of) work, Bobby could be my sidekick. Bobby certainly had the butt for it—his farts were enough to make the birds fall out of the sky, and for the government to send out the men in their "hazmat" suits to evacuate the entire town. He just needed to be able to harness this amazing power.

In order for Bobby to perfect his butt burps, I had to train him. While nobody could doubt his enthusiasm and dedication to the cause, there was still a heck of a lot of work to be done before he could become a Fart Ninja.

THE STINGER

One of the first rules of the Fart Ninja is to remain unseen as much as possible. So my first task, in training Bobby and his butt, was to show him how to master the art of "The Stinger," an all-purpose fart so noxious that police forces all over America were begging The Order of The Fart Ninjas to let them use it instead of pepper spray for riot control.

In fact, I'd heard through the Fart Ninja grapevine that there had been several attempts by the Army to capture Fart Ninjas and keep them in a secret laboratory where the government could harness the power of the Stinger by strapping canisters to the Fart Ninjas' butts. Of course, this would never work, because a true Fart Ninja has complete control over his stinky emissions (which is what I am trying to train Bobby to do). If he was ever captured and forced to fart by the government, he would only let out cute little unicorn puffs instead.

No international criminal organization has ever been brought down by unicorn puffs.

PRACTICE
MAKES PERFECT

Here's what makes "The Stinger" such an effective butt blast: it involves clenching and unclenching your butt over and over, really quickly so that you're on the verge of unleashing a standard fart, and then squeezing it back up again so the noxious air gets really compressed and super concentrated. Then, when it is finally pushed out, all its fury is released with it. As soon as the green gas reaches your intended victim, their eyes fill up with tears and they're temporarily blinded.

Bobby was actually doing okay practicing this powerful technique, except that he kept making these really weird faces as he clenched and released his butt. His face looked like he was sucking a lemon with the clench part, and during the "unclench" he looked like he was asleep and having a really good dream. What's even weirder was that his entire bottom would kind of thrust up and forwards, and then would drop back down and stick out again. (Go on, admit it, you're trying it now, aren't you?)

To break these bad habits, I tried to get Bobby to practice in front of the mirror, which almost ended in disaster as he laughed at himself so much he released all his Stingers all at once and nearly blinded himself permanently.

THE MYSTICAL
FART BOMB

BFFKT!

Once Bobby had mastered "The Stinger," we moved on to "The Mystical Fart Bomb." This is a fart so potent that it can render someone unconscious within a second of it reaching their nose. In other words, it's AWESOME!

For obvious reasons, we had to train outside for this one.

"OK Bobby, the Mystical Fart Bomb is a powerful weapon designed to temporarily put the enemy to sleep. And it's called a bomb for a reason. You drop it on their heads. Like this . . ."

I jumped into the air, did a couple of Ninja spins (not at all necessary, but I like to show off) and as I was hanging in the air, I aimed a fart at Bobby's forehead. As it hit its target, it popped like a nasty green bubble and the smell exploded right in his mouth (which was open in awe at my Ninja moves), causing him to instantly fall to the ground unconscious.

When he came to a couple minutes later, I told him, "OK, you try it now."

The first time Bobby tried it, his fart bubble went off sideways into my neighbor's backyard, and hit their Chihuahua that was innocently pooping next to the rose bushes. To make matters worse, Bobby's butt actually landed on my head as he spun around out of control, followed by the rest of him. That landed me in the Emergency Room with a huge bump on my head (and the poor Chihuahua had to be rushed to the vet!).

Needless to say, Ninja Fart training is not for the faint-hearted, but we continued to practice every day because Bobby was one of the most talented apprentices in the history of The Ninja Fart Order.

THE DARK NIGHT

Once a week, Bobby and I snuck out of our houses and met in the park after dark. For weeks, we would train under cover of the night, like true Ninjas, and I taught Bobby "The Wind-Up."

This move is the ultimate Ninja move, so secretive that only I (and now Bobby) know about it—a move so deadly that villains quake in their sneakers.

I positioned Bobby in an open space in the park, took my mark and a deep breath, pressed the palms of my hands together (this helps to push a fart to the point of no return), and ran at Bobby. Once I got close enough, I cranked up the old wind turbine. As the first fart hit the floor, it propelled me forward. Each fart bounced off the ground and back up at me, making me bounce around Bobby, my extra thick fart following me and sticking to Bobby as I circled.

As the fart became stronger, it bounced me higher, until Bobby was bound in a rope of rippers and couldn't move, and I sat panting on the ground, exhausted.

"How . . . do . . . I . . . get . . . out?" gasped Bobby, either from the tightness of the stinky string holding him, or from the smell itself.

"Sorry, dude, I haven't figured that out yet."

That was one of the problems with this particular top-secret fart: I hadn't come up with an antidote yet other than time, and so we had to wait two hours for the stinky rope to loosen up and fade away so Bobby could stumble home to bed.

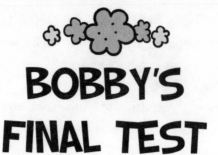

BOBBY'S FINAL TEST

Finally, after months of training, I felt like Bobby was getting close to completing his apprenticeship. However, I had to be 100 percent positive that he was ready to join the ranks of the Fart Ninjas, so there was one final test to be done.

I overheard a couple of older kids on the school bus talking about ambushing a bunch of second graders at the side entrance to the school and stealing their weekly lunch money. This was a job so big that I couldn't handle it alone, and it would be the ultimate test of Bobby's Fart Ninja abilities.

As soon as we got off the bus, Bobby and I ran as fast as we could to the other side of the school where the little kids' entrance was and hid in a tree right in front of the door. We had just enough time to pull on our masks before those big, dumb bullies arrived: Peter Oswald Oliver (or POO for short) and his cronies, Stephen Skidmark and Lee Thalgas. This was going to be easy.

LET THE
BATTLE BEGIN!

Bobby and I hid in the tree and watched as these three stupid fart-heads planted themselves right below us. Soon we saw a bunch of second graders get off their bus and start walking towards the entrance in a straight line.

As they arrived at the entrance, Peter jumped in front of them and shouted in his best movie tough-guy voice: "Give us your money and nobody gets hurt, you stupid little turds!"

At that moment, Peter's equally moronic bully buddies took a couple steps forward to stand on either side of him. We had them all right where we wanted them. I motioned to Bobby, and with perfect timing, we each dropped a Mystical Fart Bomb on Stephen Skidmark's head, who immediately fell over and hit the ground hard.

After that I leapt into the air and started bouncing around Peter, wrapping him up in my unbreakable stinky Wind-Up as I went. Then POO turned around just in time to receive a face full of Bobby's perfectly executed Stinger, which immediately blinded him.

Of course the little second graders had no idea what was going on and just stood there staring with their mouths open.

"I'd close my mouth and get inside if I was you," said Bobby, trying to sound all mysterious, like some big movie superhero that just saved a bunch of citizens from a crumbling skyscraper falling on their heads.

BOBBY, FART NINJA

As the second graders all ran into the school, we jumped back into the tree to hide until we were sure we could take off our masks without being seen.

Stephen Skidmark and Lee Thalgas had regained consciousness, and were staggering back the way they came. Peter Oswald Oliver was still bound by the Wind-Up.

"Man, that was some fancy farting you did, Milo!" said Bobby admiringly, as he high-fived me. I smiled.

"It'll wear off soon enough," I said, hopefully.

Peter looked ridiculous—with his arms pinned to his sides by ropes of stinky green gas and tears running down his face. Just as a teacher poked his head out of the school entrance to see what all the noise was about, the last of the Wind-Up holding Peter prisoner disappeared, releasing him in a final puff of fumes. Peter ran off, the teacher took one sniff and quickly shut the door, and Bobby and I were able to climb down from the tree undetected.

After that, I knew that Bobby's training was finally complete and it was time for us to go out on our first mission as two Fart Ninjas—farting for the forces of good. I knew we were going to make an awesome team.

TWO FARTS ARE BETTER THAN ONE!

And so the very next day, Bobby and I went out on a mission.

It was a pretty serious situation, but the two of us handled it pretty easily: There was a gang of bad guys smuggling farts across the border so that they could take down the Mexican government. Bobby and I focused our power and created an army of fart dragons that flew through the air. They swallowed up the gang one at a time and farted them out. The bad guys were so stunned by the smell that the police got there in time to put them all in jail, although the police were pretty unhappy that they had to put so many stinky people into their cars.

"You know what, Milo? We make a pretty good team." Bobby said.

"You know what, Bobby? We really do."

A police officer came running up to us.

"Thank you so much, young men. You two really are great warriors. You took down that whole gang."

We thanked the officer for what he said. We really had gotten stronger over the last few months. "Who are you two? How did you do that so quickly?" he asked. We looked at each other, and then responded.

"We're fart ninjas, fighting for the forces of good and for the purity of farts. We are ancient warriors in modern times, and we fight for good using nothing but our ninja fart powers."

WE'RE ON TV!

Just at that moment, a big white van showed up, and some people jumped out. I took up my ninja stance—back turned, butt out, breath held—ready to unleash a cloud of noxious gas. The way they all jumped out of the van made me worry they were a gang of ninja kidnappers who were going to take Bobby and I to some dungeon far away to harvest our farts (just like in my dream). I did a double take at Bobby, who appeared to be posing.

"Bobby" I hissed. "Ninja kidnappers, get ready to rumble."

One of the kidnappers approached us, and I took a deep breath.

"Hello boys, nice to meet you."

What? Since when are kidnappers nice? Hmm, I knew their game, trying to disarm us with their friendliness, and just when our guard was down—*BAM!*—they would cart us away in their high-tech, de-farting chamber on wheels.

"My name is Mike Methane, and I'm a reporter with Crime Fighters Round-Up."

FAME AT LAST!

It turns out the kidnappers were, in fact, reporters that had been following our crime fighting exploits for some time. They received a tip off from a police source that we had saved the day again and raced straight to the scene. They were pretty nice actually, and bought me and Bobby a milkshake from the diner across the street. It was kind of difficult trying to drink with our masks on, so the lady in the diner brought us each a straw, and we managed to fit them underneath our masks, being careful not to reveal our identities.

It was a little embarrassing, being superheroes and drinking a milkshake through a straw, but heavy duty farting is thirsty work!

EVEN MOM DIDN'T RECOGNIZE ME!

Later that night, I was sitting at the kitchen table, eating beans on toast, when Mom put the TV on. I started spluttering as Bobby and I popped up on the screen, complete with ninja masks.

"Another crime avoided, foiled by our intrepid crime busters, the Ninja Fart Warriors." Mike Methane, the reporter, looked into the camera and spoke solemnly. "Nobody knows who they are, or where they live, but these two heroes are keeping our streets safer . . ." He broke off as one of the fart smugglers stumbled across the screen, his handcuffed hands rubbing his eyes as he coughed.

". . . and smellier."

Mom sat down next to me, grabbed the remote control, and turned up the volume.

"I wonder who they are?" Then she laughed and said, "You could be a ninja whatsit, Milo, with your own farts." She chuckled at her own joke as she cleared the plates away and started to wash up.

KEEPING A LOW PROFILE

The camera moved around the scene, showing some of the smugglers still out cold on the ground from the smell Bobby and I had blasted them with earlier. Mike Methane, the reporter, was standing next to us as he talked into the camera. "Today, the Mexican government was saved from collapse by these two unknown heroes, battling for good. Tell us, ninja warriors, how did you do it?"

Bobby was next to the reporter, and he leaned towards the microphone.

"Well, Mike, me and Mi—"

I cut him off with a jab to his ribs before he could say my name and give us away. Peter moved the microphone closer to Bobby's face. As the fluffiness of the microphone tickled Bobby's nose, he sneezed so hard that a ginormous fart blasted out of his butt so hard that it blew over the tables and chairs that were outside the diner where we'd had our milkshakes.

With all the chaos Bobby caused with his fart bomb, we managed to slip away without anyone noticing. Once around the corner, we removed our ninja costumes and masks and hid them in our bags.

"You can't tell anyone who we are, Bobby. We must protect our ninja identities with our lives." Bobby started jumping up and down, all excited.

"I know, I know. We should have ninja names! I could be . . . um . . . Ninja Bobby!" Bobby isn't too bright sometimes.

THE NAME GAME

The next day, we decided to have a day off from ninja-ing. All that farting makes you tired and we needed to recharge our fart batteries. Bobby and I thought we'd bring some snacks up into my makeshift treehouse and think about awesome, fart-worthy names for our ninja alter egos.

"It needs to be something NOT like your real name," I said to Bobby, rolling my eyes. He thought for a minute.

"Okay, how about *I* am ninja Milo, and *you* are ninja Bobby? That would *really* confuse people." He looked really pleased with his idea. I knew it was going to be a long day.

DAY OFF? HA!

The thing is, ninja fart masters are never truly off duty. So when we heard some screaming coming from underneath the tree we were in, we couldn't ignore it. After all, we were heroes!

Bobby and I crept to the edge of the tree house and peered down. Far below us some bullies were trying to steal money from a couple of small girls. Bobby and I looked at each other, and grabbed our ninja masks out of our pockets.

"Quick! Just grab a name," I yelled to Bobby, pointing to the empty potato chip bag where we'd put all the names we could think of on little bits of paper.

We both pulled names out and showed them to each other. "Are you ready Farter Starter?" I called to Bobby.

"I am, Big Fart Sweetheart," he called back.

I stood upright, hand in the air. "Hooooollldddd on. Big Fart Sweetheart? That's a terrible name and it makes me sound like a girl!"

Bobby looked at me dumbfounded. "Sorry, I couldn't think of any other names."

I sighed. "Fine, I'll be Big Fart. Just that. No Sweetheart, okay?"

BIG FART AND FARTER STARTER TO THE RESCUE

While I was busy arguing with Bobby over his stupid choice of name, the bullies were surrounding the little girls. We stood, shoulder to shoulder, and brewed up the biggest farts we could. There was enough power to lift both Bobby and I off the big tree branch next to the treehouse and land us quietly behind the bullies, so they didn't see us. But they smelled us, that's for sure.

"Eeewww . . . which one of you did that?" asked the biggest boy, looking at his friends. The other three shifted around uncomfortably.

"No way, that wasn't me!" said one of them.

The smallest one pushed him in the arm. "The one who denied it supplied it." All the while Bobby and I were standing behind them.

"Well," said the other. "Whoever smelt it, dealt it!" All three of them turned to look at the biggest boy.

"Shut up, you idiots," he said, and turned to the little girls. "Okay, gimme your money and we'll let you go." That was when Big Fart and Farter Starter sprung into action!

WHOEVER SMELT IT, DEALT IT

"Unhand them, fiend!" I cried, jumping in the middle of the group.

"Yeah, what he said!" Bobby shouted, as he followed me.

We stood, back to back, moving in a circle so we had our eyes on them at all times, crouched down low. I had no idea why we were crouching, except that I had seen it in films and it looked cool. The biggest boy laughed.

"What are you gonna do about it? Run home to Mommy?"

He pushed past me to try and grab the little girl's money. Clearly, the ninja fart masters weren't going to be able to talk their way out of this one.

"Are you ready, Farter Starter?" I shouted to Bobby, as I tensed my stomach muscles.

Bobby let out a war cry. "Fart them off, then cart them off, Big Fart!"

LET 'EM RIP!

Ah, it was a beautiful thing to watch the ninja fart masters at work. Bobby and I turned our backs on the bullies, and, at exactly the same time, we let one go. The birds flew from the trees as our farts thundered through the treetops.

I had learned through my time as a ninja fart warrior that you had to make the fart match the crime. If you wanted a big fart monster to appear, you had to make the farts long, carefully squeezing them out so that they could spread themselves into huge, awesome shapes. But in this case, we needed a way to stop the thieves from taking the little girls' pocket money. We farted out quick, strong gas and sent it into the shape of handcuffs—right around the leader's wrists. Awesome!

URGH, THE TASTE!

Taking down the leader of the gang was enough. One look at the stinky cloud-cuffs around their chief's wrists was all it took for them to turn around and run for their lives! Bobby sent some fart balls after them, just to make sure they stayed away, while I kept my eye on the fart-tied fugitive.

"GET THESE OFF ME," he yelled. He lifted his wrists to his mouth to try and use his teeth to undo them. BIG mistake! "Bblleeuugh," he spluttered, trying to get the taste of stomach gas from his mouth. I looked at Bobby.

"Cabbage?" Bobby nodded. "Yep, last night. And boiled eggs this morning." The bully turned a disgusting shade of green before passing out.

GENTLEMEN NINJAS

We escorted the little girls to their house, just to make sure the other kids weren't hanging around ready to ambush them.

As we got there, the front door opened and the mother of one of the girls ran out.

"What on earth happened?" she asked. "Mommy, Mommy, some mean boys were going to take our money, but these ninjas saved us."

The mom looked at us. "Oh, my heroes, however can I thank you?" Bobby and I bowed slightly, as we'd seen in Fart Fu movies.

"No thanks necessary, Ma'am, just doing our duty." Bobby nudged me in the ribs.

"Ha-ha, you said *doody*." I sighed. He still had a lot to learn.

THE WHOLE SCHOOL IS SUDDENLY FULL OF NINJAS

Back at school, everybody was talking about the fart ninjas on the news. Everywhere we looked, kids were wearing home-made ninja masks, and holding their breath while they tried to force a deadly fart out.

As Bobby and I walked through the hallways, all we could hear were little *pfft* noises, as kids tried to copy Farter Starter and Big Fart. One kid tried so hard that he pooped himself and had to be sent home! (To be fair, the stink did clear the corridor, so it kind of worked!)

On the way home, the bus was noisy as usual. Two of the girls were braiding each other's hair, one kid was throwing his uneaten lunch around the bus, and another kid we called Greedy Greg was picking it up off the floor and eating it. Just a typical day.

But just as we were going around a corner, Greedy Greg missed the big slice of tomato that he was trying to catch, and as the driver turned to see what all the noise was, the tomato hit him straight in the eye! He couldn't see where he was going and skidded off the road, and ended up with his back wheels in a ditch.

The two girls who were messing about with their hair started crying, and Greg politely asked the driver for his tomato back. Oh man, the whole bus was going to be in trouble tomorrow after the driver told our principal about our ride home.

NINJAS GET BUS-TED

Mumbling under his breath, our driver got out and actually tried pushing the bus out of the ditch. But no matter how hard he pushed, the bus didn't move an inch. The back wheels were stuck in nearly a foot of mud and we weren't going anywhere. One of the older kids got out and went to have a look at the back of the bus. As the driver revved the engine, the wheels spun in the mud and covered the kid in dirt. We laughed, but only until he got back on. Then we all were quiet, but it was really hard not to laugh because he looked like the swamp thing.

Bobby leaned towards me and whispered something in my ear. He was right! Of course he was! We could move the bus with our ninja fart powers! It would be risky, though, without our masks to hide our identities—we knew we had to be sneaky about it. Luckily, both Bobby and I had school lunches, and school lunches *ALWAYS* gave us gas. Lots of it. I took the front of the bus, and Bobby took the back.

IS IT A BUS OR A PLANE?

Bobby stood in the aisle at the back of the bus, and I positioned myself right up front. Nobody saw us squat down slightly. Nobody even realized that our faces were turning a matching shade of red. But they did notice the smell! As Bobby and I let out our long, slow farts, and the gas filled the bus, people started choking on the stink. A few of them tried to open the windows, but they were all stuck fast with gum that gross kids had squashed in the corners.

As they coughed, gagged, and spluttered, they hardly noticed the bus starting to move. It wasn't until they looked out of the windows that they realized the bus was floating in the air! Between Bobby's and my farts, we had created enough gas to fill the bus and lift it clean into the air like a giant bus-shaped balloon!

THE BUS BALLOON

As the bus hovered above the ditch, Bobby and I thought hard. Going straight up was no good—the bus needed to be moved forward, and then let down again.

Man, this thinking thing was hard sometimes. The bus was too high up to be able to jump out and grab the fender to pull it forwards. There was only one thing for it. Big Fart was going to have to do his stinkiest, biggest, most explosive guff yet!

"Bobby, c'mere." I gestured to him to come to where I was standing so we could talk ninja fart business without the other kids hearing.

"I need you to go to the front of the bus and cause a stink." I whispered out of the side of my mouth. Bobby grinned.

"Coooooooollllll," he said.

"What? NO! Not that kind of a stink. I mean I need you to go and distract everyone. Do something to keep them all looking at you." Bobby looked disappointed.

"Why? What are YOU going to do?" I winked at him and tapped the side of my nose.

"Wait and see, my fart ninja comrade. Wait and see."

100 MILOS PER HOUR

Bobby spent a happy few minutes at the front of the bus, amusing the boys and disgusting the girls, playing tunes by putting his hand in his armpit and flapping like a chicken. I, in the meantime, tried to force the windows near the back of the bus open. I only needed it to open a tiny bit. I finally found one, almost at the back.

I clambered up onto the seat, positioned myself, balancing on the seat backs, hoping that no one would see me, and with my butt as close to the open window as I could get, I let out one of the biggest farts of my ninja life!

The fart came out with such force that it shot the bus sideways, as if someone had lit a massive rocket under it! It was awesome! As the bus flew, I shouted to Bobby to open the doors and yelled at everyone else to open any windows they could find. Now that we were clear of the ditch, we needed to let the gas out fast.

AND HOME WE GO

The bus floated gently back down to earth, landing safely on the road. All the kids looked dazed. Nobody really knew what the heck had just happened. The driver scratched his head and wiped the tomato seeds off his face before sitting back down and starting the bus. We all cheered as it shuddered into action, and we set off on the journey home.

Bobby came and sat next to me. "That was awesome, man." I have to admit, it was one of my finer moments. The ninja fart warriors had saved the day again, and we'd done it without even being in disguise! Now *that* was the mark of a true ninja!

BACK TO NORMAL

Things were quiet on the ninja front for a while, and I was pretty happy about that. It's hard work being a superhero, defender of the innocent and producer of farts. Unfortunately, Bobby even went back to some of his old tricks.

I caught him sitting on a new kid's head on the bus the other day, and I had to remind him of the fart ninja's code of honor: Thou shalt not fart for evil. But I guess we all slip up from time to time. Occasionally we had to stop traffic with a bit of ninja fartery to let an old person across the road or to push out a ladder-shaped cloud of gas up against a tree so we could rescue a cat. But no big disasters came our way, at least until our next big adventure together . . .